A Sesame Street Toddl‹

Y0-BZK-139

# Little Ernie's ABC's

Featuring Jim Henson's Sesame Street Muppets

## By Anna Ross • Illustrated by Norman Gorbaty

## Random House / Children's Television Workshop

Copyright © 1992 by Children's Television Workshop. Jim Henson's Sesame Street Muppets © 1992 by Jim Henson Productions, Inc. All rights reserved under International and Pan-American Copyright Conventions. ® Sesame Street and the Sesame Street sign are trademarks and service marks of the Children's Television Workshop. Published in the United States by Random House, Inc., New York, and simultaneously in Canada by Random House of Canada Limited, Toronto, in conjunction with the Children's Television Workshop.

*Library of Congress Cataloging-in-Publication Data*
Ross, Anna. Little Ernie's ABC's / by Anna Ross ; illustrated by Norman Gorbaty. p. cm. – (A Sesame Street toddler book)
Summary: Rhyming text takes Sesame Street characters through the alphabet, from Apple to Zebra. ISBN 0-679-82240-2
1. Alphabet rhymes. 2. Children's poetry, American. [1. Alphabet. 2. American poetry.] I. Gorbaty, Norman, ill. II. Title. III. Series.
PS3568.0841985L57 1992 811'.54–dc20 [E] 91-27823

Manufactured in Italy 10 9 8 7 6 5

*Can you say your ABC's, Little Ernie?*

# A a

Sure!
A is for apple,
juicy and red.

# B b

B is for Bert
in his own
snuggy bed.

# Cc

C is for cookies
and someone
to eat them.

# Dd

D is for dinosaurs!
It's sure hard
to beat them.

# Ee

E is for elephant,
and Ernie
(that's me).

**Ff**

F is for fishes
which swim
in the sea.

# Gg

G is for grouches
and goats
all in gray.

# Hh

H is for hippo.
How much
does he weigh?

HIPPOPOTAMUS

# Ii

I is for ice cream.
Isn't it good?

# Jj

J is for jacket.
This one
has a hood.

# Kk

K is for kites,
flying ever so high.

# Ll

L is for lamb,
woolly and shy.

# Mm

M is for map,
for finding
your way.

# Nn

N is for newspaper.
Read it today!

# Oo

O is for octopus,
with an arm
for each treat.

P is for pickles—
one sour,
one sweet.

# Pp

# Qq

Q is for quilt,
sewn with patches,
you know.

# Rr

R is for radios,
all in a row.

# Ss

S is for Snuffy
and scissors
that snip.

# Tt

T is for top.
It spins
on its tip!

# Uu

U is for umbrella—
red, green, and blue.

# Vv

V is for valentine.
This one's for
you.

# W w

W is for wagon
to give me
a ride.

# X x

X is for x-ray
to show
what's inside.

# Y y

Y is for yo-yo.
Can you
do this trick?

# Zz

Z is for zebra.
Just look at him
kick!

Now you've said your ABC's, Little Ernie!
Thank you!